The Dance Fairies

To my favourite pink party girl,
Becky Collaço

Special thanks to
Narinder Dhami

ORCHARD BOOKS
338 Euston Road, London NW1 3BH
Orchard Books Australia
Level 17/207 Kent Street, Sydney, NSW 2000
A Paperback Original

First published in 2007 by Orchard Books
© 2007 Rainbow Magic Limited
Rainbow Magic is a registered trademark

Cover illustrations © Georgie Ripper 2007
Inside illustrations © Orchard Books 2007

A CIP catalogue record for this book is available
from the British Library.

ISBN 978 1 84616 492 7
1 3 5 7 9 10 8 6 4 2

Printed in Great Britain

Orchard Books is a division of Hachette Children's Books,
an Hachette Livre UK company

www.orchardbooks.co.uk

Rebecca
the Rock 'n' Roll Fairy

by Daisy Meadows

ORCHARD BOOKS

www.rainbowmagic.co.uk

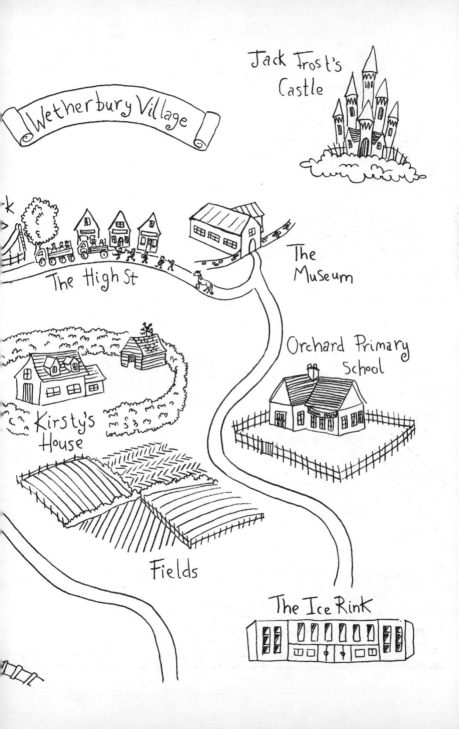

Hold tight to the ribbons, please.
You goblins now may feel a breeze.
I'm summoning a hurricane
To take the ribbons away again.

But, goblins, you'll be swept up too,
For I have work for you to do.
Guard each ribbon carefully,
By using this new power to freeze.

Contents

Rock 'n' Roll Party

"Are you ready yet, Mum?" Kirsty Tate called up the stairs. "Rachel and I are dying to see your costumes!" She grinned over at her best friend, Rachel Walker, who was standing next to her.

"We'll be down soon," Mrs Tate called back from the bedroom.

Kirsty and Rachel sat down on

the bottom stair to wait.

"I *wish* we were going to the rock 'n' roll party with Mum and Dad," Kirsty sighed. "It sounds like fun, *and* we might find Rebecca the Rock 'n' Roll Fairy's magic ribbon there!"

Rachel nodded. "The Dance Fairies are depending on us!" she reminded Kirsty.

Rachel and Kirsty had become friends with the fairies when they were holidaying on Rainspell Island, and now the girls were always eager to help whenever the fairies had a problem. The main cause of trouble in Fairyland

was mean Jack Frost, helped by his
naughty goblin servants. A few days
earlier, Jack Frost had asked the Dance
Fairies to visit his ice castle and teach his
goblins how to dance. But it was all
a trick, so that the goblins could steal
the Dance Fairies' magic ribbons!

When the King and Queen of
Fairyland had demanded that the ribbons
be given back, Jack Frost had refused.
Instead he'd sent seven of his goblins
tumbling into the human world, each
clutching one of the ribbons.

Now, during their
half-term holiday,
Kirsty and Rachel
were helping the
Dance Fairies to
find their ribbons.

"We've made a good start," Kirsty
remarked. "We've already found
Bethany the Ballet Fairy's ribbon, and
Jade the Disco Fairy's too."

"But if we don't find the rest, all the
other kinds of dancing will keep on
going wrong, and dancing won't be
fun any more!" Rachel sighed.

"Yes, and I suppose the dancing at the
rock 'n' roll party tonight will be spoiled
since Rebecca's Rock 'n'
Roll Ribbon is still
missing," Kirsty replied
with a worried frown.
"Bethany told us that
the magic ribbons are
attracted to their own kind
of dancing, remember?" Rachel
pointed out. "So maybe the goblin who

has Rebecca's ribbon will be at the rock
'n' roll party himself!"

"Girls, we're ready!" Mr Tate yelled
from upstairs and Kirsty and Rachel
turned round.

Mr and Mrs Tate came downstairs,
and the girls' eyes widened with delight.
Kirsty's dad was wearing jeans and
a black leather jacket, and his hair was
gelled into a quiff at
the front. Kirsty's
mum was wearing
a white circular
skirt, embroidered
with black musical
notes and a black
top. She had a high
ponytail, which was
tied up with a red ribbon.

"You both look *fantastic!*" Kirsty gasped.

"You look like you just walked out of the film *Grease!*" Rachel added. "Will everyone be dressed up like you?"

Mr Tate nodded. "There's also going to be demonstrations of rock 'n' roll dancing," he explained, "and an Elvis Presley impersonator. Elvis was a famous rock 'n' roll singer, you see."

"And Kirsty's Uncle John is in charge of the music," Mrs Tate told Rachel. "We're taking some of our own rock 'n' roll records for him to play."

"It sounds like fun," Kirsty said wistfully.

"Well, why don't you two come

along?" Mrs Tate suggested with a smile. "We didn't ask you before because there aren't going to be any other young people there, but you might enjoy it."

Kirsty and Rachel looked thrilled.

"Can we?" Kirsty asked eagerly. "But what about Gran? She was going to come and look after us."

"She won't have left home yet," Mrs Tate said, glancing at the clock. "I'll give her a ring."

"Does it matter that we don't have costumes?" asked Rachel.

"Not at all," Mr Tate assured her.

"Isn't this great?" Kirsty whispered to Rachel as they went to grab their coats.

"We're going to the rock 'n' roll party after all!"

"Yes, and maybe we'll find Rebecca's Rock 'n' Roll Ribbon!" Rachel replied excitedly.

Rebecca in a Spin

After Mrs Tate had rung Kirsty's gran, they all set off for the village hall where the rock 'n' roll party was being held. As they walked inside and took off their coats, the girls looked eagerly around. Everyone was dressed up in rock 'n' roll outfits, and rock 'n' roll music was playing in the background. The hall

was filled with round tables and
chairs, apart from a large space
in the middle which had been
kept free for dancing,
and there was also
a refreshments table
selling food and
drink. At the
opposite end of
the hall was
a brightly-lit stage.

"Who's *that*?"
Rachel asked
curiously, pointing to
a man on the stage
who was busy setting
up a microphone. The
man had dark hair and
bushy sideburns, and he was

wearing a sparkly white jumpsuit. "Oh, that's the Elvis impersonator," Mrs Tate explained. "He'll be singing later on." "We'll pick up some drinks and snacks for us all and then find a table," said Mr Tate. "Would you girls mind taking these records over to John? He's over there by the record decks." Mr Tate handed the box of records to Kirsty and then

he and Mrs Tate went to join the
queue at the refreshments table.

Meanwhile, Rachel and Kirsty made
their way across the hall. The record
decks, connected to some very large
speakers, were set up next to the stage,
and boxes of records had been laid out
in neat rows, but there was no sign of
Kirsty's uncle.

"I wonder where Uncle John is?"
Kirsty remarked.

"I'm right here!" A fair-haired man who looked very similar to Mr Tate popped up from under the table. "I was just fixing a loose wire. How are you, Kirsty?"

"I'm fine, Uncle John." Kirsty grinned, handing over the box of records. "This is my friend Rachel."

"Ah, the famous Rachel!" Uncle John exclaimed. "I've heard a lot about you! Excuse me for a moment, girls," he

went on quickly, "I must get the next record ready to start."

Kirsty and Rachel watched as Uncle John put another record on one of the decks.

"Ladies and gentlemen!" came an announcement at that moment. "May I have your attention please?"

There was a burst of applause and Kirsty and Rachel swung round to look up at the Elvis impersonator on the stage. "I'd like to welcome you all to our rock 'n' roll party!" Elvis went on. "We've got a fantastic night's entertainment lined up. And first on stage

are Linda and Will Melling, who are going to show us how to dance rock 'n' roll style."

As Linda and Will walked onto the stage in their sparkly rock 'n' roll outfits, the girls exchanged a worried glance.

"I hope their dance goes OK without the magic ribbon," Kirsty whispered.

"Yes, I'm crossing my fingers!" Rachel whispered back.

Uncle John lowered the needle onto the record and the music began. The song had a very fast beat, and Linda and Will started off by holding hands and doing a complicated series of steps involving lots of twists and turns around the stage.

"I don't know anything about rock 'n' roll dancing, but this looks great to me!" Rachel murmured to Kirsty.

But right at that moment Linda suddenly stumbled. She managed to regain her balance quickly and smiled brightly at the audience, but the next second Will tripped, stubbing the toes of his left foot on the floor.

"Ow!" he yelled, and then quickly looked very embarrassed.

Linda tried to cover up the mistake by twirling across the stage in front of him, but unfortunately she stepped clumsily on Will's other foot as she did so.

"Ouch!" Will gasped.

"Oh, no!" Kirsty groaned as Will and Linda danced on, looking rather red. "This is all because Rebecca's ribbon is missing!"

Rachel nodded. The girls watched anxiously, hoping nothing else would happen, but it soon became clear that neither Linda nor Will could remember their steps. Linda went left when she should have gone right, Will went right when he should have gone left, and they ended up bumping heavily into each other. Then, as Linda jumped into Will's arms and he tried to lift her above his head, they collapsed in an ungainly heap on the stage.

The audience looked shocked and the Elvis impersonator rushed out of the wings to help the dazed dancers to their feet. After a murmured conversation between the three of them, Elvis grabbed the microphone again.

"Linda and Will are going to take a quick break," he announced, looking rather flustered. "They'll be back for another performance later on."

Looking very embarrassed, Linda and Will fled from the stage as everyone applauded politely. Kirsty and Rachel felt very sorry for them.

"I don't understand it!" Uncle John said in confusion, as he put another record on. "Linda and Will are usually brilliant! Maybe one of them is feeling ill or something. I'll just pop backstage and check they're OK." He slipped out from behind the record decks. "Will you girls keep an eye on things for me?" he asked. "I'll be back before this record finishes."

The girls nodded and Uncle John hurried off.

"Poor Linda and Will," Kirsty sighed. "This is all because of mean old Jack Frost and his goblins!"

"Hello!" called a tiny, silvery voice suddenly.

Rachel grabbed Kirsty's arm. "Did you hear that?" she gasped.

Kirsty nodded. "But where's it coming from?" she asked, glancing around.

"I'm down here!" the voice called.

Rachel and Kirsty looked down at the record decks. There, sitting on the edge of the record that was spinning around on the turntable, was a tiny, sparkling fairy.

"Oh!" Kirsty exclaimed. "It's Rebecca the Rock 'n' Roll Fairy!"

A Glimpse of Goblins

"Hi, girls!" called Rebecca, beaming all over her pretty face. She wore a purple scoop-necked top, a circular black skirt embroidered with big pink spots, and a matching pink scarf around her neck. Her long brown hair was tied up in a ponytail, just like Mrs Tate's.

"Hi, Rebecca!" Rachel and Kirsty

whispered as the little fairy fluttered daintily off the spinning record.

"What are you doing here?" added Kirsty eagerly. "Is your ribbon nearby?"

Rebecca nodded. "I think so," she said in a low voice. "I can *feel* it, but it can't be very close, otherwise poor Linda and Will wouldn't have danced so badly."

Rachel and Kirsty nodded. They knew that when a magic ribbon was very close by, everyone danced beautifully.

"Girls, we must find the ribbon before Linda and Will go back on stage," Rebecca said in a determined voice.

"Then my lovely rock 'n' roll dancing will be perfect! Will you help me look for the goblin? He must be around here *somewhere*."

"Of course we will," Kirsty replied. But just then she saw Uncle John heading back towards them. "Rebecca, here comes my uncle! You'd better hide."

Rebecca immediately flew to hide on Rachel's shoulder behind her hair.

"Looks like Will and Linda are absolutely fine now," Uncle John said cheerfully.

"I've just watched them practising backstage, and they were brilliant! I think they must have had a bad attack of nerves earlier."

"This is very strange!" Rebecca whispered to Rachel. "My ribbon's missing, but Will and Linda are dancing properly again. That can only mean one thing…"

"…the ribbon's backstage!" Rachel finished for her in a low voice.

Kirsty heard her and looked excited. "Let's go backstage right away, then, and find the goblin!" she whispered.

36

There was a door at the
side of the stage and
the girls made their
way over to it,
leaving Uncle
John to put on
another record.

They were
worried that
someone might
notice them, but
luckily people were too
busy chatting and buying
refreshments. Quite a few couples were
already on the dance floor, including
Mr and Mrs Tate. But just like Will
and Linda, they all kept bumping into
each other, treading on toes and
forgetting their steps.

"This party will be a disaster if I don't find my ribbon!" Rebecca sighed as Kirsty opened the door.

Rebecca, Rachel and Kirsty found Will and Linda practising their moves in a room behind the stage. The two dancers seemed like a different couple from the clumsy, awkward duo who had performed earlier. Now their kicks and twirls were completely in time and they didn't make a single mistake.

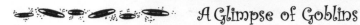

"Uncle John was right!" Kirsty said admiringly, as Will flipped Linda high up into the air and then caught her again. "They are amazing!"

"My ribbon is in here somewhere!" Rebecca said eagerly. "I can sense it!"

Rachel glanced around and suddenly noticed that one of the cupboard doors behind them stood slightly ajar. As she stared at it, she saw a knobbly green foot poke out through the gap, just for a second, before it quickly disappeared again.

"Kirsty! Rebecca!" Rachel whispered excitedly. "There's a goblin inside that cupboard!"

Goblins Revealed!

"Are you sure?" Rebecca asked.

Rachel nodded. "I saw his foot poking out," she explained.

"We can't do anything about the goblin while Will and Linda are here," Kirsty said. "We'll have to wait until they've finished practising."

The girls watched as Will and Linda

worked on their finale. Will threw
Linda up into the air again, where she
turned a double somersault and landed
in Will's arms before lowering herself
into the splits.

"That's much better!" Will beamed
at his partner. "I don't know *what*
went wrong before."

"Yes, it was *so* embarrassing!"
Linda groaned.

"Let's get a drink before we go back on stage," Will suggested, and they hurried off, giving the girls a friendly smile as they went.

Immediately Rebecca flew out from behind Rachel's hair and the three friends dashed over to the cupboard.

"Be careful, Kirsty!" Rachel warned as her friend reached for the door handle. "Remember that Jack Frost has given the goblins freezing powers!"

Carefully Kirsty pulled the door open and the girls peered inside.

The cupboard was crammed with music stands, old props from plays, and *two* goblins squashed one behind the other. The goblin at the front was clutching a sparkly purple ribbon in his hand.

When they saw the girls the goblins both let out a loud shriek of annoyance.

"Go away!" yelled the one with
the ribbon, trying to pull the door
closed again. "You can't see us!
We're hiding!"

The other one scowled, grabbed the
head from a pantomime
horse and put it
over his own
head. "Now
you can't
see me!" he
said in
a muffled voice.
"Go away!"

But Kirsty shook her head firmly.

"I'm not going anywhere until I get
my magic ribbon back!" Rebecca said,
hovering in the doorway.

The first goblin looked nervous.

"Don't come near me!" he shrieked.
"I don't want to be frozen!"

Rachel, Kirsty and Rebecca glanced at each other in confusion. "You idiot!" the second goblin said, pulling the horse's head off and poking his friend hard in the ribs. "*We're* the ones who can freeze people as long as we have a magic ribbon, *not* them!"

"Oh, yes!" said the first goblin, "I forgot." Then his face darkened. "And don't poke me or I'll poke you harder!"

Rachel was staring at the second

goblin. "That's the goblin who stole Bethany's Ballet Ribbon!" she whispered to Kirsty.

"I think he's recognised us too!" Kirsty whispered back as the second goblin glared at them.

"Never mind about me!" the second goblin yelled as the first goblin gave him a sharp poke in the ribs. "You should be freezing the pesky fairy and her human friends."

"Ooh, yes!" said the first goblin eagerly.

"I'll turn you into fairies, girls," Rebecca called, quickly lifting her wand as the first goblin lunged out of the cupboard towards them.

"Go on, freeze them all!" the second goblin sniggered, tumbling out after his friend.

A shower of magic dust from Rebecca's wand fell softly around Rachel and Kirsty and transformed them into fairies in the twinkling of an eye. Immediately the girls fluttered their gauzy wings and flew up into the air out of the goblin's reach.

"Oh, I *hate* it when they do that!" the

first goblin said crossly. He started
jumping up into the air, trying to touch
Rachel, Kirsty and Rebecca and shouting
"Freeze!" but he missed every time.

"What shall we do now?" Rachel
asked as they hovered above the
goblins' heads. "We still have to get the
ribbon back somehow."

"It's going to be hard with two
goblins," said Rebecca anxiously.

Kirsty frowned at the two goblins below. The first one was still leaping up and down and shouting "Freeze!" at them, although they were well out of his reach.

"Maybe we could get the first goblin to freeze the second one?" she suggested. "We just have to make sure they're touching each other when the first goblin says 'Freeze!'."

"That's a great idea!" Rebecca said with a big grin. "Let's lead them into it. On the count of three – one, two, three!"

Linking hands, Rachel, Kirsty and Rebecca immediately flew down and hovered near the second goblin. With a shriek of triumph the first goblin rushed towards them. The girls waited until the last possible moment and then zoomed upwards out of reach.

"Freeze!" shouted the first goblin, just as he collided heavily with his friend.

The Magic Singing Stick

Instantly the second goblin was frozen solid. The first goblin landed on the ground and his frozen friend fell over too, and landed in his lap. The first goblin looked so shocked, the girls and Rebecca couldn't help laughing.

"Oh, no!" the first goblin groaned, pushing his frozen friend off him so that he could stand up. Then he stood the second goblin up too and examined him carefully. He poked and prodded him hard. He even tried breathing warm air onto him, but it was no use. The second goblin remained completely frozen, an expression of surprise on his face.

"So now we only have *one* goblin to deal with!" said Rebecca. "How shall we make him give my ribbon back?"

Before the girls could answer, they heard the sound of music coming from the stage behind them. The Elvis impersonator had started singing and the slow, beautiful melody caught their attention.

"Oh!" Kirsty said suddenly, "I know this! It's a famous song by Elvis Presley called *Love Me Tender*. My dad plays it all the time."

"I think the goblin likes it too!" Rachel whispered.

The first goblin had stopped trying to thaw out his friend. Instead he was swaying to the music, his head cocked on one side, an expression of enchantment on his face.

"I've never heard such beautiful music!" he said dreamily, waving the magic ribbon and beginning to dance.

"He can't help but dance to rock 'n' roll music while he's

holding my ribbon," Rebecca laughed as the goblin danced his way closer to the back of the stage. "We'd better go after him, girls!"

"What about the frozen goblin?" asked Rachel, "We can't leave him here. Somebody might come along and see him!"

Rebecca waved her wand and the frozen goblin floated gently into the air and into the props cupboard, the door closing behind him. The other goblin was now standing in the wings, still swaying dreamily and staring in awe at the Elvis impersonator.

"Love me tender," the goblin croaked loudly, trying to sing along.

"He's terrible!" Rachel whispered.

"We must stop him before someone hears!" Kirsty added urgently.

"Just be careful because he can still freeze us," Rebecca warned as they zoomed towards the goblin. "Although I think the music has made him forget all about his freezing powers."

The girls and
Rebecca hovered
around the
goblin's head,
but he didn't
even notice
them until
Rebecca tapped
him on the shoulder
with her wand.

"It's better if you just listen," said
Rachel. "Elvis will stop singing if he
thinks everyone wants to sing instead of
listening to him."

The goblin shut up immediately.
"I don't want him to stop," he
sighed happily.

"Do you like singing?" asked Kirsty.
The goblin nodded. "But goblins

aren't any good at singing," he said in a sad voice. "I think it's because we don't have magic singing sticks like the man on the stage."

"Magic singing sticks?" Kirsty repeated, confused.

"Yes, *all* the best singers have them!" the goblin said impatiently. "I've seen them on TV in the human world."

"He means a microphone," Rachel whispered. And as she said that, an idea popped right into her head. Quickly she drew Rebecca and Kirsty aside.

"We can see how much the goblin wants to sing like Elvis," she

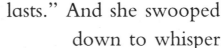

pointed out. "Rebecca, do you think
you could magic up a microphone that
makes everyone who sings into it sound
like Elvis? I'm sure the goblin would
swap the magic ribbon for *that*!"

"Of course I can!" Rebecca nodded.
"The microphone won't last for ever,
though. It will dissolve into fairy dust
after a few hours."

"That should be long enough," said
Rachel. "I'm sure the goblin will have
lots of fun with the microphone while it

lasts." And she swooped
down to whisper
in the goblin's
ear. "Would
you like to sound
like Elvis?"
Rachel asked.

The goblin nodded eagerly.

"Well, we can give you a magic singing stick of your very own!" Kirsty joined in. "Follow us!"

Rebecca and the girls led the goblin right away from the stage and into an empty room. First Rebecca scattered purple fairy dust over Rachel and Kirsty to make them human again. Then, with another flick of her wand, a tall, shining silver microphone appeared in a burst of purple sparkles.

"Oh!" The goblin clapped his hands in delight. "How does it work?"

Rachel went over to the microphone. "You sing into this bit and it makes you sound like Elvis," she explained.

Rachel sang *Love Me Tender* into the microphone and was rather surprised when her voice came out deep and manly and just like Elvis Presley's, right down to the American accent!

Kirsty and Rebecca laughed.

"Ooh! I want it!" the goblin shrieked excitedly, jumping up and down. "Give me the magic singing stick RIGHT NOW!"

Rockin' Goblin

"We'll swap the magic singing stick for the magic ribbon," Kirsty said. "But you know this kind of fairy magic doesn't last for ever. In a few hours it'll dissolve away into fairy dust."

The goblin barely hesitated. "That's OK," he said, shoving the ribbon at Rachel and grabbing the

microphone stand.

Rebecca gave a little squeal of delight. She immediately shrank the ribbon down to its Fairyland size and it floated out of Rachel's hand to reattach itself to her wand. As it did so, the ribbon glowed a deeper shade of purple and was briefly surrounded by a faint mist of lavender sparkles.

Just then the second goblin rushed into the room.

"He's thawed out!" Rachel whispered. "We got the ribbon back just in time!"

The second goblin glared at his friend. "Why has that pesky fairy got her ribbon back?" he demanded.

"I swapped it for this magic singing stick!" the first goblin explained, stroking the silver microphone proudly.

"What?" shrieked the second goblin furiously. "What's Jack Frost going to say when he finds out you've swapped the magic ribbon for a silly silver stick?"

"It's not silly!" the first goblin snapped indignantly. "Listen!" And he began to sing.

The second goblin looked very impressed when he heard his friend's wonderful Elvis voice. "I want a magic singing stick!" he declared jealously, trying to grab the glittering microphone. "It's mine!" the first goblin roared furiously.

And, picking up the microphone, he dashed off with the other goblin in hot pursuit.

"I think that's the last we've seen of them for tonight!" Rebecca laughed. "Girls, I simply can't thank you enough. You've been amazing!" She grinned happily at Kirsty and Rachel. "And now I must go straight back to Fairyland and tell everyone the good news!"

Just then they heard the sound of applause from the hall.

"Linda and Will are back on stage," Rebecca went on. "And their rock 'n' roll dance should go well now that I've got my ribbon back." She waved her

wand at the girls and the magic
ribbon sparkled. "Good luck
with finding the other
ribbons, and keep
a sharp look-out
for more goblins,
girls!" Rebecca
called, and
then she
vanished in
a puff of
purple sparkles
as the girls
waved goodbye.

Kirsty and
Rachel rushed back
into the hall to join
Mr and Mrs Tate. They
were just in time to see

Will and Linda launch into
a very complicated routine
of steps, kicks and
twists which they
performed with
perfect timing,
neither of
them missing
a beat. Then
Will lifted
Linda high
over his head
and there was
a gasp of
amazement from
the audience as she
jumped right over
him and landed neatly
on the other side.

Rachel and Kirsty grinned at each other.

"Everything's fine now that Rebecca's got her rock 'n' roll ribbon back," Rachel whispered.

"But there are still *four* ribbons to find," Kirsty pointed out with a smile. "I wonder what our next fairy adventure will be?"

The Dance Fairies

Rebecca the Rock 'n' Roll Fairy has got her magic ribbon back. Now Rachel and Kirsty must help

Tasha the Tap Dance Fairy

BETHANY
THE BALLET FAIRY
978-1-84616-490-3

JADE
THE DISCO FAIRY
978-1-84616-491-0

REBECCA
THE ROCK 'N' ROLL FAIRY
978-1-84616-492-7

TASHA
THE TAP DANCE FAIRY
978-1-84616-493-4

JESSICA
THE JAZZ FAIRY
978-1-84616-495-8

SASKIA
THE SALSA FAIRY
978-1-84616-496-5

IMOGEN
THE ICE DANCE FAIRY
978-1-84616-497-2

Win Rainbow Magic goodies!

In every book in the Rainbow Magic Dance Fairies series (books 50-56) there is a hidden picture of a ribbon with a secret letter in it. Find all seven letters and re-arrange them to make a special Dance Fairies word, then send it to us. Each month we will put the entries into a draw and select one winner to receive a Rainbow Magic Sparkly T-shirt and Goody Bag!

Send your entry on a postcard to Rainbow Magic Dance Fairies Competition, Orchard Books, 338 Euston Road, London NW1 3BH. Australian readers should write to Hachette Children's Books, Level 17/207 Kent Street, Sydney, NSW 2000.
New Zealand readers should write to Rainbow Magic Competition, 4 Whetu Place, Mairangi Bay, Auckland, NZ. Don't forget to include your name and address. Only one entry per child.
Final draw: 30th September 2008.

Good luck!

Have you checked out the

website at:
www.rainbowmagic.co.uk

by Daisy Meadows

The Rainbow Fairies

The Weather Fairies

The Party Fairies

The Jewel Fairies

India the Moonstone Fairy	ISBN	978 1 84362 958 0
Scarlett the Garnet Fairy	ISBN	978 1 84362 954 2
Emily the Emerald Fairy	ISBN	978 1 84362 955 9
Chloe the Topaz Fairy	ISBN	978 1 84362 956 6
Amy the Amethyst Fairy	ISBN	978 1 84362 957 3
Sophie the Sapphire Fairy	ISBN	978 1 84362 953 5
Lucy the Diamond Fairy	ISBN	978 1 84362 959 7

The Pet Keeper Fairies

Katie the Kitten Fairy	ISBN	978 1 84616 166 7
Bella the Bunny Fairy	ISBN	978 1 84616 170 4
Georgia the Guinea Pig Fairy	ISBN	978 1 84616 168 1
Lauren the Puppy Fairy	ISBN	978 1 84616 169 8
Harriet the Hamster Fairy	ISBN	978 1 84616 167 4
Molly the Goldfish Fairy	ISBN	978 1 84616 172 8
Penny the Pony Fairy	ISBN	978 1 84616 171 1

The Fun Day Fairies

Megan the Monday Fairy	ISBN	978 184616 188 9
Tallulah the Tuesday Fairy	ISBN	978 1 84616 189 6
Willow the Wednesday Fairy	ISBN	978 1 84616 190 2
Thea the Thursday Fairy	ISBN	978 1 84616 191 9
Freya the Friday Fairy	ISBN	978 1 84616 192 6
Sienna the Saturday Fairy	ISBN	978 1 84616 193 3
Sarah the Sunday Fairy	ISBN	978 1 84616 194 0

The Petal Fairies

Tia the Tulip Fairy	ISBN	978 1 84616 457 6
Pippa the Poppy Fairy	ISBN	978 1 84616 458 3
Louise the Lily Fairy	ISBN	978 1 84616 459 0
Charlotte the Sunflower Fairy	ISBN	978 1 84616 460 6
Olivia the Orchid Fairy	ISBN	978 1 84616 461 3
Danielle the Daisy Fairy	ISBN	978 1 84616 462 0
Ella the Rose Fairy	ISBN	978 1 84616 464 4

The Dance Fairies

Bethany the Ballet Fairy	ISBN	978 1 84616 490 3
Jade the Disco Fairy	ISBN	978 1 84616 491 0
Rebecca the Rock'n'Roll Fairy	ISBN	978 1 84616 492 7
Tasha the Tap Dance Fairy	ISBN	978 1 84616 493 4
Jessica the Jazz Fairy	ISBN	978 1 84616 495 8
Saskia the Salsa Fairy	ISBN	978 1 84616 496 5
Imogen the Ice Dance Fairy	ISBN	978 1 84616 497 2

Holly the Christmas Fairy	ISBN	978 1 84362 661 9
Summer the Holiday Fairy	ISBN	978 1 84362 960 3
Stella the Star Fairy	ISBN	978 1 84362 869 9
Kylie the Carnival Fairy	ISBN	978 1 84616 175 9
Paige the Pantomime Fairy	ISBN	978 1 84616 209 1
Flora the Fancy Dress Fairy	ISBN	978 1 84616 505 4
The Rainbow Magic Treasury	ISBN	978 1 84616 047 9
Fairy Fashion Dress-Up Book	ISBN	978 1 84616 371 5
Fairy Friends Sticker Book	ISBN	978 1 84616 370 8
Fairy Stencils Sticker Colouring Book		978 1 84616 476 7
Fairy Style Fashion Sticker Book		978 1 84616 478 1

Coming soon:

Chrissie the Wish Fairy	ISBN	978 1 84616 506 1

All priced at £3.99.
*Holly the Christmas Fairy, Summer the Holiday Fairy, Stella the Star Fairy,
Kylie the Carnival Fairy, Paige the Pantomime Fairy, Flora the Fancy Dress Fairy* and
Chrissie the Wish Fairy are priced at £5.99. *The Rainbow Magic Treasury* is priced at £12.99.
Rainbow Magic books are available from all good bookshops, or can be ordered
direct from the publisher: Orchard Books, PO BOX 29, Douglas IM99 1BQ
Credit card orders please telephone 01624 836000
or fax 01624 837033 or visit our Internet site: www.orchardbooks.co.uk
or e-mail: bookshop@enterprise.net for details.

To order please quote title, author and ISBN and your full name and address.
Cheques and postal orders should be made payable to 'Bookpost plc.'
Postage and packing is FREE within the UK
(overseas customers should add £2.00 per book).
Prices and availability are subject to change.

Look out for the Sporty Fairies!

HELENA
THE HORSERIDING FAIRY
978-1-84616-888-8

FRANCESCA
THE FOOTBALL FAIRY
978-1-84616-889-5

ZOE
THE ROLLERBLADING FAIRY
978-1-84616-890-1

NAOMI
THE NETBALL FAIRY
978-1-84616-891-8

SAMANTHA
THE SWIMMING FAIRY
978-1-84616-892-5

ALICE
THE TENNIS FAIRY
978-1-84616-893-2

GEMMA
THE GYMNASTICS FAIRY
978-1-84616-894-9

Available
April 2008